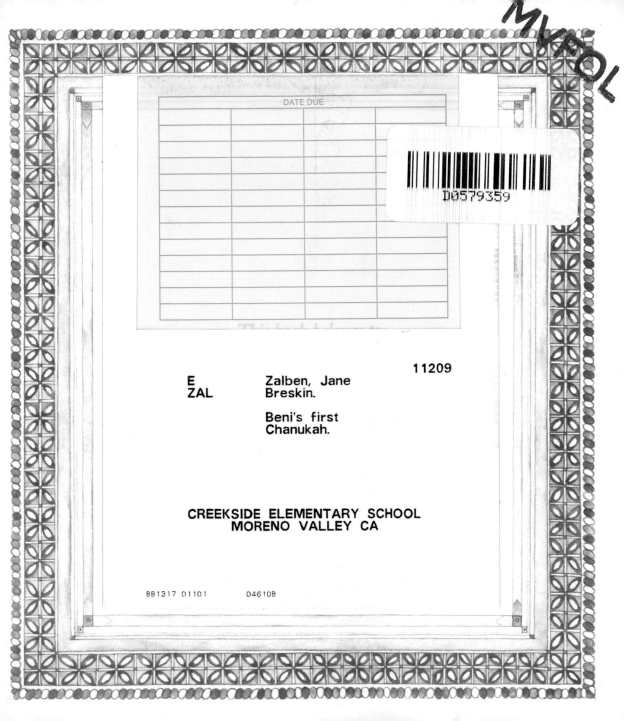

DATE DUE

D0579359

11209

E
ZAL

Zalben, Jane
Breskin.

Beni's first
Chanukah.

CREEKSIDE ELEMENTARY SCHOOL
MORENO VALLEY CA

8B1317 01101   04610B

Beni's First Chanukah

STORY AND PICTURES BY
JANE BRESKIN ZALBEN

HENRY HOLT AND COMPANY
New York

Copyright © 1988 by Jane Breskin Zalben
All rights reserved, including the right to reproduce this book or portions thereof in
any form. Published by Henry Holt and Company, Inc., 115 West 18th Street, New York,
New York 10011. Published in Canada by Fitzhenry & Whiteside Limited,
195 Allstate Parkway, Markham, Ontario L3R 4T8.
Library of Congress Cataloging-in-Publication Data
Zalben, Jane Breskin. | Beni's first Chanukah.
Summary: On the first night of Hanukkah, a young
bear helps his mother prepare latkes, plays "Spin the
Dreidel," and recites a prayer with his father.
[1. Hanukkah—Fiction   2. Bears—Fiction] I. Title.
PZ7.Z254Be 1987   [E]   86-33634
ISBN: 0-8050-0479-3
Henry Holt books are available at special discounts
for bulk purchases for sales promotions, premiums,
fund-raising, or educational use. Special editions
or book excerpts can also be created to specification.
For details contact:
Special Sales Director
Henry Holt & Co., Inc.
115 West 18th Street
New York, New York 10011
Designed by Jane Breskin Zalben
Printed in the United States of America
5 7 9 10 8 6 4

To Ben and Sara

 The morning air was cold.
Beni sank deeper under the quilt,
and curled his paws with excitement.
At sunset, it would be the first night of Chanukah, the
first Chanukah Beni would be old enough to remember.

After breakfast, Beni helped Mama peel potatoes for latkes.
His sister, Sara, made applesauce for the pancakes.
The kitchen smelled of fresh cinnamon and lemon rind.

Sara spooned sour cream into Mama's best bowl
and Beni helped Papa fry jelly doughnuts.
Sugar powdered their noses.

The rest of the morning, Beni and Sara
searched for their Chanukah presents,

one for each of the eight nights,
but they found nothing.

Light flakes of snow began to dust the trees.
Beni and Sara pressed their noses against the
windowpanes, hoping they could play in the flurry.
Mama said, "Dress warmly."
Papa wrapped them in long woolen scarfs.

Sara tried to make snowballs, but they fell apart.
Beni laughed. "They look like Mama's potato pancakes!"
And they pretended to eat them.

"Let's visit Sasha and Christopher," Beni said.
Sara followed him down the hill, finding treasures
along the way. And so did Beni.

When they got to their friends' house, Beni placed
a special pinecone on the lower bough of Sasha and
Christopher's tree. Sara reached as high as she could,
and nestled some red winter berries in a branch above.
They all made a star out of twigs and put it on the top
of the tree. The pink-and-orange sky glowed on a mound
of snow. Beni and Sara returned home, inviting Sasha and
Christopher to their house.

When nighttime came, the whole family arrived—
grandparents, aunts, uncles, and cousins.
Beni emptied a box of colored candles.
Beni chose his favorite color,
yellow, and green for the shammas.
Papa picked up Beni in his arms,
and held the bright green candle.
Beni repeated the prayer after Papa.
Mama smiled proudly.

The light from the menorah warmed
the frosted sill outside. Beni and Sara
taught Sasha and Christopher how to
spin the dreidel. Everybody sang songs.
Then it was time for the gifts.

Sara got hers first. Then she helped her
little brother and cousins unwrap their presents.
Beni got just what he always wanted.
Sasha and Christopher each untied a bag
of chocolate gold coins.

Everyone sat around the fire.
Grandpa told the story of Chanukah, about
how the oil burned magically for eight nights.
Beni pretended to be a Maccabee warrior.

As the first night of Chanukah came to an end,
Sasha and Christopher said, "It was wonderful."
Beni asked his parents, "Could they come the
second night too?" Mama and Papa nodded yes.

At bedtime, Beni's parents kissed him goodnight
and said, "Happy Chanukah!"
Beni held his new stuffed bear a little tighter.
"This was my best Chanukah ever."
Sara tiptoed in. Mama and Papa hugged Beni
and whispered, "It was ours too."

Mama's Latkes

4–5 large potatoes   ¼ cup matzoh meal
1 medium onion   salt and pepper
2 large eggs   vegetable oil

1. Peel potatoes, wash in cold water, grate finely.
2. Grate onion on larger side of grater.
3. Beat 2 eggs and add to mixture.
4. Blend in matzoh meal, and salt and pepper to taste with other ingredients.
5. Heat 1″ layer of vegetable oil in large frying pan. Drop in 1 heaping tablespoon of mixture for each latke, and when it sizzles turn over until it's crisp and golden.
6. Drain on paper towels.
7. Serve with sour cream or applesauce.

Serves about 6 people, depending on their appetites! Beni eats 4 pancakes. He loves his Mama's latkes.

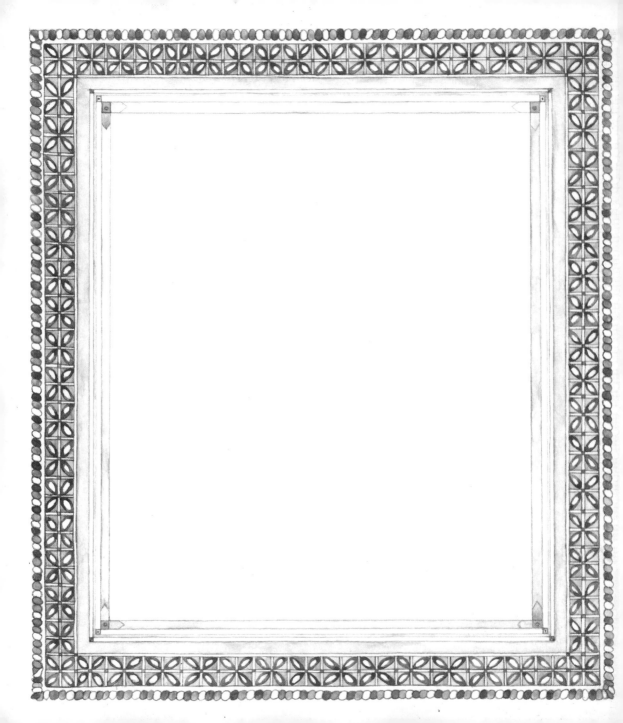